21st Century Junior Library

Healing Plants

by Jennifer Colby

CHERRY LAKE PUBLISHING * ANN ARBOR, MICHIGAN

Published in the United States of America by Cherry Lake Publishing
Ann Arbor, Michigan
www.cherrylakepublishing.com

Consultants: Elizabeth A. Glynn, Youth Education Coordinator, Matthaei Botanical Gardens and Nichols Arboretum, University of Michigan; Marla Conn, ReadAbility, Inc.

Photo Credits: © lzf /Shutterstock Images, Cover, 8; © Botamochy/Shutterstock Images, 4; © Marina99/Shutterstock Images, 6; © kostrez/Shutterstock Images, 10; © George Dolgikh/Shutterstock Images, 12; © Mrsiraphol/Shutterstock Images, 14; © sybanto/Shutterstock Images, 16; © Mr Twister/Shutterstock Images, 18; © Tim Mainiero/Shutterstock Images, 20

LIBRARY OF CONGRESS CATALOGING-IN-PUBLICATION DATA
Colby, Jennifer, 1971-
Healing plants/by Jennifer Colby. - [Revised edition]
pages cm.—(21st century junior library)
Includes bibliographical references and index.
ISBN 978-1-63188-037-7—ISBN 978-1-63188-123-7—
ISBN 978-1-63188-080-3—ISBN 978-1-63188-166-4
1. Medicinal plants–Juvenile literature. I. Title. II. Series: 21st century junior library.
QK99.A1C65 2014
581.6'34–dc23 2014006225

Cherry Lake Publishing would like to acknowledge the work of The Partnership for 21st Century Skills. Please visit www.p21.org *for more information.*

Printed in the United States of America

CONTENTS

Some of these plants can make you feel better.

Plants for Many Purposes

There are many kinds of plants. Some plants grow tall and leafy. Others have pretty flowers. Some plants grow food we can eat.

Did you know that some plants help us feel better when we are sick?

Different parts of the dandelion can make you feel better.

Some plants have liquids that can help our skin. Some plants are used to make healthy teas. Some plants are used to make medicines. Let's take a closer look at some plants that heal.

Think!

There are many kinds of teas at the store. Look at the **ingredients** on the box. Were plants used to make the teas?

The aloe vera plant is used to make lotion to help soothe sunburn.

Leaves and Flowers

The **aloe vera** plant has thick, green leaves. The leaves have sharp edges. When the leaves are cut, a clear, thick liquid comes out. This liquid is used to help heal skin problems.

Chamomile flowers are used to make a healing tea.

Chamomile is an **herb**. Herbs are used in cooking or for making medicines. Chamomile flowers have small, white petals. They have large, yellow centers. The flowers are used to make tea. The tea can help people sleep. It can also ease an upset stomach.

Create!

Grow a healing plant. Buy ginger root from the store. Soak it overnight. Ask an adult to cut it into a few pieces. Plant the pieces in a pot with dirt in it. Place the pot in a warm spot. Give it water every day. Soon ginger shoots will grow.

The ginger plant is used for healing.
It is also used to flavor food.

Stems and Bark

The part of the ginger plant that people use grows under the ground. This part is not a **root**. It is a special kind of stem.

The ginger stem is used to flavor many kinds of foods. You may have tasted ginger. Have you ever eaten gingerbread cookies? Have you ever had ginger ale?

Ginger ale can help an upset stomach feel better.

Ginger is often used to ease **nausea**. If you have an upset stomach, you may have nausea. Ginger can help your stomach feel better.

Make a Guess!

A **recipe** for a meal may contain ginger. Do you think your family uses ginger? Ask the person who cooks your next meal if ginger is one of the ingredients.

A medicine used as a pain reliever comes from the bark of willow trees.

Other parts of plants can make you feel better. **Quinine** is made from the bark of the cinchona tree. Quinine is used to treat **malaria**. Malaria causes a high fever. People with malaria can take quinine to help them feel better. A doctor must write a **prescription** for quinine.

Ask Questions!

A **pharmacist** prepares and sells medicines. Do you want to know more about plants that heal? Ask your pharmacist to tell you about medicines that contain plants.

Lily of the valley smells good. But don't eat it! It can make you very sick.

Plant Safety

Some plants can help people when they are sick. Other plants can make you sick. Some plants are **poisonous**. Do not eat these plants. Some plants should not be touched. It is hard to tell the difference between safe and unsafe plants.

Don't touch poison ivy. It will make your skin red and itchy.

Plant medicines are like any other medicines. You should always ask an **expert** before using any medicine. Doctors, nurses, and pharmacists will answer your questions. They will tell you about plants that heal.

Look!

Look in the yards or parks around you. Can you find plants that heal? Do you see plants that look strange? Ask an adult to help you get information about the plants you find.

GLOSSARY

aloe vera (AL-oh VAH-ruh) a plant with thick, green leaves that have prickly edges

chamomile (KAM-uh-mile) a kind of flowering plant

expert (EK-spurt) a person with a high degree of skill in or knowledge of a certain subject

gingerroot (JIN-jur-root) the scented underground stem of the ginger plant

herb (URB) leaf or flower of a plant used in cooking and medicine

ingredients (in-GREE-dee-uhnts) things that are used to make something

malaria (muh-LAIR-ee-uh) a disease spread by mosquitos that causes a high fever

nausea (NAW-zee-uh) a feeling of being sick to your stomach

petals (PET-uhlz) parts of a flower that are usually brightly colored

pharmacist (FARM-uh-sisst) a person who prepares and sells medicines

poisonous (POI-zuhn-uhs) capable of causing death or illness if eaten

prescription (pri-SKRIP-shuhn) an order from a doctor that tells a pharmacist what kind of medicine to give a patient

quinine (KWI-nine) a medicine that comes from the bark of a tree and is used to treat malaria

recipe (RES-uh-pee) the instructions and list of ingredients for making food

root (ROOT) the part of a plant that grows underground and soaks up water and minerals

FIND OUT MORE

BOOKS

Doudna, Kelly. *Mischievous Mosquitoes. Minneapolis*: ABDO Publishing Co., 2012.

Morgan, Sally. *How We Use Plants for Medicine and Health. New York*: PowerKids Press, 2009.

WEB SITES

National Geographic—Edible and Medicinal Plants

http://channel.nationalgeographic.com/channel/doomsday-castle/galleries/edible-and-medicinal-plants/at/acorns-1680327
Photos and descriptions of plants that can be eaten or used to heal.

Centers for Disease Control and Prevention—Bam! Body and Mind

www.cdc.gov/bam
Learn about fitness, food and nutrition, exercise, disease, and safety. Take a quiz or play a game.

INDEX

ABOUT THE AUTHOR

Jennifer Colby is a school librarian, and she also has a bachelor's degree in Landscape Architecture. By writing these books she has combined her talents for two of her favorite things. She likes to garden and grow her own food. In June she makes strawberry jam for her children to enjoy all year long.